My Butt is SO CHRISTMASSY!

Dawn McMillan

Illustrated by
Ross Kinnaird

Dover Publications
Garden City, New York

It's Christmas Day tomorrow!
Our house is filled with delight.
I'm **skipping** and **flipping**, **jumping** and *dipping*,
because …

Santa is coming tonight!

My big sister is wearing her new holiday sweater.
And Auntie is eating crackers and cheddar.
Uncle says he would like pizza better.

Grandma and Pops brought lots of **surprises**
Wrapped in boxes of all different sizes.

And
of course
my cousins
are here!

My cousins are **mischievous!**

They **jump** all about.
They make **rude** noises
And they laugh and they shout.

But I sit here, keeping quiet as a mouse,

While Mom and Dad are like **elves**, filling the shelves,
And sweet Christmas smells drift through the house.

Our tree looks amazing with **bells** and a **star**.
It *twinkles* with blue and red light.
It's bright and it's **cheery** but I'm feeling dreary
because ... suddenly ... I know ...

that something about me isn't right!

It's my butt, can't you see—it doesn't suit me.
It's not in a **Christmassy** mood.

It's just a plain butt, in pants that are RED.
But I'd like a fancier butt instead.

I want to wear something exciting and **bold!**

Something festive ... like ...

Tinsel! Silver and gold!
My butt will **dazzle** and glow.
And underneath ... Santa undies perhaps?
No one will ever know!

My butt will look **jolly**
wearing some holly,
but ... what if I have to sit?

There'll be *eeking* and **shrieking**,
squawking and **squeaking** ...

I need something softer,
something easy to wear,
like **long** Christmas stockings
to *hang* here and there.

I'd like some sparkles,
Shining so bright.
And reindeer and snowflakes
That glow in the night.

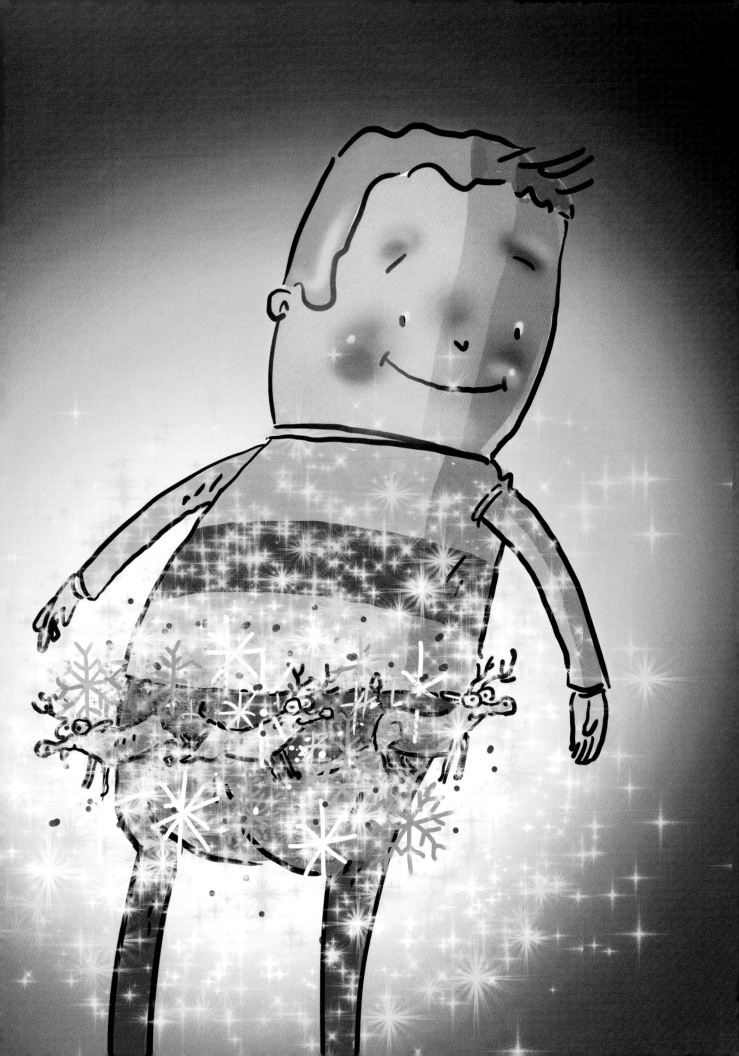

A Christmas tree! Now that will suit me.
With layers and layers of green.
With **baubles** that glow, bows in a row,
and a star where it's easily seen.

Bells will be great, to jingle all day.
Angels and snowflakes to make a display.
My butt will be stunning!
A joy to behold …

But suddenly ...

I think about Christmas, the story we're told.
And I know ...
Yes, my thoughts are quite clear.
Christmas is a very **special** time of year!

It's all about **love** and family
For caring and sharing ...
and *not* all about me ...

So ...

I'll just be the boy in RED pants tonight.
I'll take a deep breath. I'll be *polite*.
I'll **smile** as I think of what my butt could be
If what I was wearing was left up to me.

It's Christmas morning ... **Santa** was here!
He left me a gift by the tree.
It's light! It's lumpy! So **soft** and bumpy ...

I squeeze and I **prod**. What can it be?

I gasp. I **shout**. I jump all about!
"Perfect!" I say. "What a delight!"
And then I think …

How did Santa get my present
so right?

About the author

Hi, I'm Dawn McMillan. I'm from Waiomu, a small coastal village on the western side of the Coromandel Peninsula in New Zealand. I live with my husband, Derek, and our cat, Lola. I write some sensible stories and lots of crazy stories! I love creating quirky characters and hope you enjoy reading about them.

About the illustrator

Hi. I'm Ross. I love to draw. When I'm not drawing, or being cross with my computer, I love most things involving the sea and nature. I also work from a little studio in my garden surrounded by birds and trees. I live in Auckland, New Zealand. I hope you like reading this book as much as I enjoyed illustrating it.

Bibliographical Note

This Dover edition, first published in 2022, is an unabridged republication of the work published as *My Bum is SO CHRISTMASSY!* by Oratia Media Ltd., Auckland, New Zealand, in 2022. The text has been Americanized for this edition.

International Standard Book Number

ISBN-13: 978-0-486-85069-6
ISBN-10: 0-486-85069-2

Manufactured in the United States of America
85069201   2022
www.doverpublications.com